Dick and Jane

READING COLLECTION • VOLUME 11

We Play

GROSSET & DUNLAP • NEW YORK

Table of Contents

Play

Oh, Father.

See funny Dick.

Dick can play.

Oh, Mother.

Oh, Father.

Jane can play.

Sally can play.

Oh, Father.

See Spot.

Funny, funny Spot.

Spot can play.

See Dick Play

Look, Jane.

Look, look.

Look and see.

See Father play.

See Dick play.

Look, Mother.

Look, Mother, look.

See Father.

See Father and Dick.

Oh, Mother.

See Spot.

Look, Mother, look.

Spot can help Dick.

Funny Spot

Come Spot.

Come, come.

Play Spot.

Play, play.

Go, Spot.

Go, go.

Spot can play.

Dick can play.

Oh, oh.
Funny, funny Spot.

See Spot Play

See Jane jump.

Jump, jump.

See Spot jump.

Jump, jump.

Oh, Dick.

Oh, Jane.

See Spot.

Funny, funny Spot.
Spot can play.

Funny Father

"Come, Jane," said Father.
"Come and play ball.
Come and play."

"I can help you play ball," said Father.
"I can help."

"Come, Father," said Jane.
"Come and play ball.
Come and play."

Oh, funny, funny Father.

Play Ball

"Come, Jane," said Father.
"Come and play ball.
Come and play."

"Oh," said Jane.
"See the red ball go.
See it go up, up, up.
Run, Dick, run."

"Oh, oh," said Dick.
"Where is my ball?
I can not find it.
Come here, Jane.
Run and help me.
Help me find my red ball."

"I can help you," said Jane.
"We can find the red ball."

Dick said, "I see it.
I see my red ball.
Look, Father.
See where it is.
Come and help me."